ELIJAH & PIN-PIN

RAOUL MILLAIS

SIMON & SCHUSTER BOOKS FOR YOUNG READERS
Published by Simon & Schuster
New York · London · Toronto · Sydney · Tokyo · Singapore

For Robin, Mark and Lorna

SIMON & SCHUSTER BOOKS FOR YOUNG READERS
Simon & Schuster Building, Rockefeller Center,
1230 Avenue of the Americas, New York, New York 10020

First published in Great Britain 1991 by ABC, All Books for Children,
a division of The All Children's Company Ltd.
First U.S. edition 1992

Copyright © 1991 by Raoul Millais

SIMON & SCHUSTER BOOKS FOR YOUNG READERS
is a trademark of Simon & Schuster

Manufactured in Hong Kong

10   9   8   7   6   5   4   3   2   1

Library of Congress Cataloging-in-Publication Data
Millais, Raoul, 1901-
Elijah and Pin-Pin / by Raoul Millais
p. cm.
Summary: Elijah the mole invites Pin-Pin the hedgehog
to a house-warming party with disastrous results.
[1. Moles (Animals) — Fiction. 2. Hedgehogs — Fiction.
3. Animals — Fiction. 4. Friendship — Fiction.] I.Title.
PZ7.M603El 1992   [E] — dc20   91-20032   CIP   AC

ISBN 0-671-75543-9

This is the story of

Elijah   and Pin-Pin.

Elijah was a mole who lived under a castle. Pin-Pin
was a hedgehog who lived in the forest nearby.

Elijah wore a velvety gray-black coat and had large,
strong hands for digging underground passages. These
passages led to rooms under the castle, where he lived

with Mrs. Elijah and their four children. To make his castles (or molehills), Elijah collected all the earth from his tunnels and carried it upstairs and out into the field.

The farmer who owned the field didn't like the castles much and kicked them over. Elijah would wait for him to go away and then carry more earth upstairs to make new castles. But even more than making castles, Elijah loved snaffling up the hundreds of worms that wriggled across the pathways he tunneled.

Glowworms were his favorites, yet he never ate them. They came out at night and burned like bright little lanterns in the grass. Elijah discovered that if he tied them on long strings and hung them from the ceiling, they lit up all the dark passages in his castle. He called these glowworm chandeliers, and liked to boast that he had invented them. On the first warm day of the year, Elijah finished his biggest and best castle. He bustled into the kitchen to tell Mrs. Elijah.

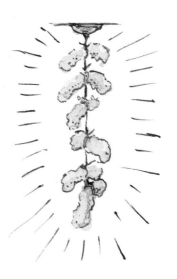

"It's wonderful! My most brilliant idea yet! No more cold bedrooms for you, my dear. I've burrowed right underneath the farmer's compost heap, so our little room should stay warm and cozy. I've even moved our leaf mattress from the old bedroom. Don't you have a clever husband?" he asked.

"Yes, I'm very proud of you, Elijah," replied his wife. "We must have a party to celebrate. Let me see, I'll need to . . . oh, be careful!"

But it was too late. Elijah had knocked a can of worms off the table and onto the floor, where they wriggled off in every direction. Quickly, Elijah snuffled around the kitchen until he had gobbled up every last worm. He looked up and saw Mrs. Elijah's angry face.

"I think old Pin-Pin might wake up today," he muttered. "I'll go and see if I can find him." And with that, Elijah hurried out of the castle.

Pin-Pin was rather fat and had hundreds of prickles on his back. When he was in danger, he rolled himself into a tight ball and lay very still. The prickles kept his enemies away. Sometimes, fierce dogs came into the forest, barking and snarling as they rushed at him. If a dog had tried to bite Pin-Pin once, it would never try a second time. Pin-Pin's sharp spikes would prickle the dog's wet nose, causing the unfortunate animal to run off howling, with its tail between its legs.

Pin-Pin slept all winter under a great pile of oak leaves. But now it was spring. Snowdrops and yellow aconites pushed up through the grass, nodding their heads at Elijah as he made his way up the forest path. The sun was shining. Elijah felt very hot in his black velvet coat.

He pulled out his spotted handkerchief, mopped his brow, and looked for a nice pile of leaves, where he could sit down and cool off. At that moment, Pin-Pin woke up. He yawned, stretched, and arched his back—just as Elijah sat down! Elijah leaped into the air with a yell.

Pin-Pin rolled out of bed. "Oh, I'm terribly sorry, Elijah. I had no idea you were going to sit down on me."

"You should put up a red flag when you're sleeping, Pin-Pin," moaned Elijah. "Now I've got a sore bottom! I might feel a bit better after a little something to eat, though. I believe it's very good for shock."

"I think you're right," replied Pin-Pin. "I'm pretty hungry, too, after that long sleep. Let's go for a walk and see what we can find. A beetle sandwich would be nice, I think, or perhaps a snail pie." He smacked his lips at the thought.

Like Elijah, Pin-Pin had four children. Mrs. Pin-Pin spent hours washing and brushing them (prickly work with hedgehogs) because she liked taking them to lots of parties and picnics. That same afternoon, she was passing Elijah's castle with her children when up popped Mrs. Elijah.

"Hello there," she called. "Where are you off to? I'm giving a castle-warming party today, and I've been so busy getting ready that I haven't had time to invite any guests. Please come. But I can see you're going shopping. I know, why don't you leave the children here until you come back?"

The little hedgehogs were very excited. "Oh, please, may we stay? Please!"

"All right, but be good," said Mrs. Pin-Pin. "Thank you, Mrs. Elijah. It's kind of you to offer. I'll leave them while I go and meet Auntie." So the four children scampered up the side of the castle and disappeared down the entrance to find their mole friends.

At that moment, Auntie herself hurried up, carrying her shopping basket. A bulgy red umbrella protruded from under her arm. She wore a large straw hat trimmed with flowers and feathers, and looked very untidy and out of breath. "Have you heard?" puffed Auntie. "There's been an accident in the forest. I just happened to overhear Mrs. Blackbird telling Miss Thrush about it. It seems Fred has been seriously hurt. The birds flew off before I could catch anything else, so I don't know exactly what happened; but the doctors are there, and Elijah and Pin-Pin are doing their best to help."

Fred was a rabbit who liked playing practical jokes on his neighbors and trying to frighten them. One day he rushed out of a hole, terrifying poor Auntie so much that she lost her spectacles and couldn't find them for a week. Everyone used to say that something should be done about Fred or there would be an accident. And they were right, of course. This is how it happened.

It was all Nuts's fault, really. Nuts was a red squirrel without a thought in his head. He would collect hazelnuts, hide them in holes in trees, and then forget where he had put them. Fred always teased him. "You're an even bigger fool than you look, and that's pretty difficult," he taunted.

This afternoon, Nuts thought it was time to show Fred that the rabbit had met his match. Nuts found a large walnut left over from autumn and heaved it up a tall fir tree that grew next to the path Fred always took. He stretched out along an overhanging branch and waited. In the distance, Nuts saw Fred flopping along, singing at the top of his voice:

"I'm so very clever
That I never, never, never
Get found out.
I terrify the ladies
And petrify their babies
When I bound out.
Old Nuts is so half-witted
That he's only to be pitied.
What a . . . "

C L U N K !

Fred didn't finish his song because Nuts dropped the walnut onto his head. Fred saw all the stars in the heavens, then dropped to the ground, unconscious. "Hee, hee! That'll teach him a lesson," giggled Nuts.

But Fred lay so still that Nuts began to worry. "Suppose he's dead . . . "

Nuts began running up and down the tree, chattering feverishly, "I must get help. I must find the doctors." He dashed off into the darkest part of the forest.

The doctors were two old owls called To-whit and To-who. There had been a third one called To-what, but he had gone off in a huff after squabbling with the others about a vole. Owls often do that.

While Nuts was looking for the doctors, Elijah and Pin-Pin were walking along the grassy path, deep in conversation. Elijah was telling Pin-Pin about all that the hedgehog had missed during his long winter sleep. As they came round the bend, they nearly fell over Fred.

"What's this?" cried Elijah.

"It's Fred and he's dead," whispered Pin-Pin.

"This is no time for poems," said Elijah. "We must get help at once!" Seeing the large lump between Fred's ears, Elijah pulled out his spotted handkerchief and carefully bound up Fred's head with it.

At that moment, To-whit and To-who silently sailed down beside him.

"Thank goodness," said Elijah. "There's been a very serious accident here. But where are your black bags, your pills, and your medicine bottles?"

To-whit and To-who said nothing, but walked slowly round Fred several times, puffing up their feathers and trying to look very wise.

"Come on, come on, come on," said Elijah impatiently. "Attend to Fred, or he'll be dead. He's got a big lump on his head."

"Now who's making up poems?" grumbled Pin-Pin.

"Silence, if you please," said To-whit and To-who together, glaring at Elijah and Pin-Pin.

To-whit slowly drew a black bottle and a large spoon from under his wing. "This is our hooting mixture," he said, "guaranteed to cure all ills, from the snuffles to the pip: headaches, faceaches, tummyaches, and toothaches; footsores, jigsaws, seesaws, and cat's-paws; measles, freezles, and fainting weasels; mumps, frumps, and umpty tumps. . . ."

"Just a minute, please," said Elijah, holding up one of his large hands. "You don't seem to understand. Fred has been severely banged on the head. He hasn't got any of your silly diseases. You must wake him up. At once, please!"

To-whit and To-who put their heads together and began whispering to each other. "We have it!" they cried. "The very thing — *Bunny's Balsam*: specially made for bangs and bumps; it sometimes even cures the blues. Balsam clears up ugly lumps. It's also good for chimney flues."

"Goodness me!" thought Pin-Pin. "Now *they've* started making up poems."

To-whit produced another bottle. To-who pulled out a large feather. He approached Fred on tiptoe and tickled him until he began to wriggle and giggle.

"He's alive, he's alive!" cried Elijah and Pin-Pin.

"Hush," said the doctors. "We mustn't wake him too quickly — the shock, you know."

The more they tickled him, the more Fred squirmed. At last, he opened his mouth and began to roar with laughter. Still his eyes were shut tight. To-who quickly dipped the feather into the bottle of balsam and shoved it down Fred's throat. Spluttering, coughing, hiccuping, and wheezing, Fred blinked his eyes open.

"Hurrah, hurrah, he's cured!" they all cried.

By this time, Nuts was back, looking very embarrassed. "I promise never to do it again . . . until the next time," he added to himself.

"Do what?" they all asked.

"Oh, nothing," said Nuts, scampering away quickly and pretending to look for something.

"What did he mean?" said Fred, untying the spotted handkerchief.

"Who knows?" replied Elijah. "He's not called

Nuts for nothing. Now, let's all go back to my castle for tea. My wife is giving a castle-warming party, and I know we can rely on her to put out a good spread."

"That's not a bad idea," said Fred, who seemed to have recovered somewhat. "But I'm not coming if Nuts is."

"Now then," said Elijah, "you two must make up and be friends. It's absolutely no good for the two of you to fight like this."

"Well, I suppose you're right," Fred agreed. He didn't really mean it, but he knew Elijah would just keep telling him off otherwise.

Mrs. Elijah had seated all the children at the long table in the kitchen. Spread out in front of them were piles of delicious food: beetle cake, worm sandwiches, slug pie, and a large pot of snail tea.

"Now then, children, eat up," said Mrs. Elijah. "When you've finished, we'll have a dance."

"Hurrah!" they all squealed. Then they stuffed themselves with food until their tummies were nearly bursting.

Mrs. Elijah popped the last worm sandwich into her mouth, then threw open the doors of the big cupboard in the corner. What a surprise! Out scrambled a huge band of mice, each carrying a different musical instrument. They jumped onto a low bench and started to play a lively jig.

The children pushed aside the table and cleared the floor. Screaming with joy, they bounced up and down to the music. Each little mole took a little hedgehog as a partner. They were very careful not to bump into one

another, as the moles weren't eager to be prickled! The band played louder and louder, everyone danced faster and faster, and the glowworm chandeliers shivered and shook from the thumping of paws on earth.

The eldest Pin-Pin had eaten far too much. He fell onto the drum and punctured several holes in it. The mouse drummer was furious and beat the hedgehog with his tiny drumsticks.

In the confusion, no one noticed a wisp of smoke curling under the door to the passageway. Suddenly, there was a loud crack, and the door split from top to bottom. A tongue of flame licked into the room. The children screamed with terror and Mrs. Elijah fainted.

Panic overtook the mouse band. *"Fire, fire! Help, help!* We're trapped. We shall all be suffocated!" they squeaked.

Only the bandleader kept his head. "Look!" he shouted. "There's a big trapdoor in the ceiling and a long ladder in the corner. We can all escape if we just keep calm."

The oldest mole child brought the ladder and propped it up against the wall below the trapdoor.

"Now then," shouted the bandleader. "One at a time, up you go. There's no need to rush, you'll all get out. And don't forget your instruments, you mice."

The drummer went up first. He pushed open the trapdoor, letting in a rush of fresh air that revived Mrs. Elijah. Spluttering and coughing, she managed to herd all the children up the ladder. Just as she was about to step onto the bottom rung, Mrs. Elijah remembered that she had left a bowl of water in a corner. Bravely, she went back into the smoke, seized the bowl, and sloshed it onto a pile of flaming leaves.

The compost heap had started to smolder, and some

glowing twigs had fallen through the castle's thin ceiling. Mrs. Elijah's bed of dry leaves had caught fire easily.

"Dear, dear," she sighed, looking at the now-soggy mess. "Back to freezing cold bedrooms, I suppose." At the top of the ladder, several small faces peered down into the darkness to see what was happening. Mrs. Elijah scrambled up to join them just as fast as she could.

Elijah, Pin-Pin, Fred, Nuts, and the doctors were making their way slowly down the path to Elijah's castle. Elijah was fanning himself with his spotted handkerchief. Pin-Pin, hungrier than ever, was poking about, shoving his nose under stones, looking for fat beetles and snails. Fred and Nuts were quarreling as usual. There was still a lump on Fred's head.

"I wish I could remember what happened," said Fred. "I have a strange suspicion that *you* had something to do with it, Nuts."

"Er, no-no-no, indeed no, not me!" said Nuts. "I, er, um, er, I didn't drop a walnut on your head at all . . . no." Nuts felt rather nervous because everybody suddenly took great interest in what he was saying. So, changing the subject quickly, he said, "Look at that funny cloud over there."

Everyone stopped and stared. An enormous plume

of smoke was rising from one of Elijah's castles.

"Oh! Oh! My house, my house!" yelled Elijah. "It's on fire. Quickly! Help, help!"

They all ran as fast as they could across the field. Fred was there first, then Nuts, followed by Pin-Pin and Elijah.

"Not our business, really," grumbled To-whit, "but perhaps we'd better go in case anyone is hurt. It might look rather bad if we didn't."

"I suppose you're right," said To-who, and they waddled slowly after the others.

The wormskin hose that Mrs. Elijah had sewn for her husband was hanging on a tree by the forest pool. "Follow me!" Elijah shouted. "We'll soon get the hose working."

Despite the confusion, Elijah had noticed To-whit and To-who smacking their beaks and glaring greedily at the mouse band scurrying toward the pool. Owls are crazy about mice, so you can imagine how excited they were at seeing so many mouse dinners. To-whit secretly fancied the fat trumpeter, and To-who was beadily eyeing the concertina player.

"Now, you two, behave yourselves," warned Elijah. "Promise me you won't touch any of those mice."

"Oh, bother and blow!" said To-who. "I knew he'd spoil our fun."

"I didn't want to come, anyway," added To-whit, and they both strutted off.

Meanwhile, the others had reached the pool. Nuts scampered up the tree and tossed the hose down from the broken twig on which it hung. The mice put one end in the water and raced down the hill toward the fire with the other end. Elijah was still only halfway up the hill and feeling rather out of breath, but he began giving his orders: "Fred! Nuts! Sit on the hose near the pool to stop the water from coming down. I'll shout when we're

ready for it."

"Right," called Fred. "Did you hear that, Nuts, or are you deaf, as well?"

"If you're going to be rude, I won't help," twittered Nuts. But he went over and sat on the hose, anyway.

Back at the castle, the littlest mole and the youngest hedgehog were still feeling scared and couldn't help sniffling. Mrs. Elijah was trying to comfort them, while Auntie and Mrs. Pin-Pin were busy making sure that nobody had frazzled his fur or scorched her spines. Auntie, who was rather shortsighted, did not notice the mouse band rush past carrying the wormskin hose. When she tripped over the hose, she had no idea what it was, so she held up the end to have a closer look.

At that very moment, Elijah trod on a thistle. He let out a yell that could be heard a mile away. Fred and Nuts jumped off the hose, thinking it was Elijah's signal to let the water run. The water rushed very fast and burst with a tremendous *whoosh* into Auntie's face. Away went her spectacles, her straw hat, her red umbrella, and her shopping basket. Auntie lay on her back, soaking wet, her legs flapping feebly in the air.

When they saw what had happened, Fred and Nuts rushed back to stop the torrent. Fred was bubbling with laughter, thinking it the best practical joke ever.

"Look what you've done, you fools," roared Elijah in a terrible rage. "You've nearly drowned poor Auntie. You two can't be trusted with even the simplest task!"

Just then, To-whit and To-who swooped down beside him. They had heard Elijah's yell and reluctantly decided to see if they were needed.

"Ah, good, I was wondering where you were," said Elijah. "Please attend to Auntie, will you? I have some very important work to do." This was quite true. Elijah was desperate to save his precious glowworm chandeliers.

Smoke still billowed out of the new castle. An ominous rumbling noise came from underground. Fire roared along the passageways.

Elijah steeled himself. "Here goes," he said, and launched himself down the entrance to the castle. (It had caved in, so Elijah had to tunnel through.) As he dug deeper and deeper, he felt hotter and hotter, and the rumbling grew louder and louder.

Suddenly, with a great BOOM, the castle exploded and Elijah was shot high into the air. Great flames flared from the hole where his castle had once

been. But Elijah picked himself up and hurried back for the hose.

When they heard the loud bang, Fred and Nuts leaped off the hose again. But this time it was exactly the right thing to do. Elijah snatched up the hose and directed a great jet of water into the passage.

Slowly, the fire began to die down. There were loud hissings and gurglings far below. Elijah's spotted handkerchief, which had been on fire, was now smoldering quietly in his pocket. Of course, Fred noticed this and chuckled, but on no account was he going to mention it.

By now, Auntie had drunk a bottle and a half of hooting mixture, and felt much better. She tipsily tottered up and fished the handkerchief out of Elijah's pocket with the point of her umbrella. Then she turned round and belted Fred over the head with the umbrella.

"That'll teach you! How dare you laugh at poor Elijah. He ought to have a medal for what he has done," Auntie cried, then promptly toppled — *plop* — into a pool of water.

Fred thought that was even funnier than the handkerchief, but this time he didn't dare laugh.

Elijah held up his hand for silence and started to speak: "On behalf of my wife and children, as well as myself, I would like to thank you all, especially the bandmaster, for your splendid behavior at this very trying time." Blowing out his cheeks and puffing up his chest, he beamed at everyone present.

"Oh, help!" sighed Mrs. Pin-Pin. "Here comes one of Elijah's awful long lectures. I can't stand it."

Pin-Pin had known Elijah for long enough to understand exactly what his wife meant. He crept up from behind and hugged Elijah so tightly that the mole could not say a word.

"My dear fellow, please don't tire yourself anymore," said Pin-Pin. "You must be exhausted, and we are all very hungry and thirsty. I suggest we have a party up here in the field. There's plenty of food. I have already sent one of the children for my secret store of beetles, and there's a whole jam jar full of worms just for you."

Elijah was spluttering and wheezing, trying to

escape from Pin-Pin's hug, but he couldn't. Every time he struggled, Pin-Pin squeezed him harder. He finally gave up and stood quietly panting, unable to say another word.

Mrs. Elijah, followed by some of the mouse band, went down the ladder into the kitchen. Although there was a strong smell of smoke, the fire had done very little damage to most of the castle. And, best of all, the glowworm chandeliers still shone brightly. Mrs. Elijah found a large tablecloth, which she gave to the mice. They ran up the ladder with it and spread it on the grass outside. Mrs. Pin-Pin tied a long string to Auntie's shopping basket and lowered it down into the kitchen. Mrs. Elijah filled the basket with:

bread and butter and cans of snails,
slugs and bugs and water shrimps' tails,
beetles and worms and bits of cheese,
lettuce and nuts and bumblebees,
flies and ants and dozens of berries,
apples and pears and bowls of cherries.

Mrs. Pin-Pin pulled up the basket and laid everything out on the tablecloth. By now, Elijah had recovered from Pin-Pin's squeeze, and he called the whole party to gather around for the feast.

The children had guzzled so much earlier that they didn't feel very hungry. But Pin-Pin was *starving*. He hadn't eaten anything all winter. Auntie nibbled at a soggy beetle sandwich. Fred ate four lettuces and made quite a hole in a huge cabbage. Naturally, the mice polished off the cheese in no time.

When everybody had eaten enough, Mrs. Elijah folded up the tablecloth. The children helped Auntie and Mrs. Pin-Pin clear up the rubbish, which they buried in a vacant rabbit hole.

But what about the doctors? To-whit and To-who had been disappointed about the mouse band, though they realized it was bad manners to eat fellow guests. Instead, the two owls each gobbled up quite a few of the bumblebees. They flew up to a branch of the oak tree, where they could watch the celebration. But soon the bees' furry fluff tickled inside the owls' tummies so much that they began to hoot with laughter. This just made the tickling worse, so the hooting grew louder and louder. "My word," said Elijah, "what is that noise? I must go and see."

He and Pin-Pin hurried over to the tree. They looked up and saw To-whit and To-who bouncing up and down on a branch, going, "Honk-honk, hoo-hoo,

honk-honk, hoo-hoo-hiccup!" The tickling was becoming unbearable. To-whit and To-who flew shakily over to the hose. They gratefully glugged the last trickle of water seeping out of the end.

"Never again!" groaned To-who.

"No more bees!" gasped To-whit. They both looked quite ill.

"Imagine doctors making themselves sick like that," said Pin-Pin.

Elijah quickly changed the subject. "By the way, how much do we owe you for the hooting mixture you gave Auntie? And for attending to Fred?"

"Nothing, nothing, my dear fellow," said the doctors. "It's all free. Only too pleased to help. But in return, you might do us a tiny favor. We would like your delightful little friends the mouse band to come for tea tomorrow, we mean *to* tea, at our tree house. We're too shy to ask them ourselves. Would you invite them for us? Too kind." And with that the owls floated soundlessly away into the forest.

Elijah and Pin-Pin stood watching them fly into the distance.

"I'm not sure that we should do that," said Pin-Pin anxiously.

"Don't be so silly," replied Elijah. "They can always say no, can't they. That bandleader seems to have a good head on his shoulders. He won't let those mice get into any trouble."

They turned away and wandered back to the party.

The mouse band was blowing, banging, and scraping away on their instruments. The drummer seemed happy again, bashing a large empty can with his drumsticks. Fred was his old self once more and was giving dancing lessons to anyone who wanted them. Auntie had joined in and was fanning herself on top of one of Elijah's castles.

"I think we'll leave them to it," said Pin-Pin.

"Right-oh," said Elijah.

And we'll leave them, too, as they wander away, two old friends sniffing the lovely forest smells in the twilight.